This book belongs to

This edition published by Parragon Books Ltd in 2015

Parragon Books Ltd
Chartist House
15–17 Trim Street
Bath BA1 1HA, UK
www.parragon.com

ISBN 978-1-4723-8203-0

Printed in China

Disney · PIXAR MOVIE COLLECTION

A SPECIAL DISNEY STORYBOOK SERIES

Parragon

Bath • New York • Cologne • Melbourne • Delhi
Hong Kong • Shenzhen • Singapore • Amsterdam

TRIPLE-R

"Hey, Woody! Ready to go to Cowboy Camp?" Andy shouted, bursting into the bedroom.

Woody was very excited about camp, though he couldn't show his feelings to Andy. Toys were supposed to stay still whenever people could see them.

With a few minutes to spare before leaving for camp, Andy grabbed Woody and Buzz, his two favourites, for a quick adventure. Suddenly, there was a loud RIIIPPPP!

Woody's shoulder had ripped open!

Andy's mum suggested fixing Woody on the way to camp, but Andy shook his head and sighed. "No, just leave him."

"I'm sorry," his mum replied. "But you know toys don't last forever."

Sadly, Andy handed the pull-string cowboy doll to his mum, who placed Woody up on the highest shelf in the room. Then they left.

Woody was shocked by what had happened. What if Andy never played with him again?

Woody watched sadly as Andy left without him. And he didn't feel any better when he found Wheezy, a toy penguin, who'd been sitting broken and forgotten on the shelf for months. Maybe that would be Woody's future, too.

Suddenly, the toys spotted something terrifying – Andy's mum was putting up a sign outside: GARAGE SALE!

Unfortunately, she chose Wheezy as one of the sale items. Thinking quickly, Woody waited until Andy's mum was out of sight, then whistled for Buster, Andy's friendly puppy. Together, they sneaked outside, grabbed Wheezy and were heading back to safety when Woody, struggling to hold on with his injured arm, lost his grip and tumbled to the ground. Then, a strange man noticed Woody, picked him up ...

... and stole him!

From their upstairs window, the other toys watched in horror as the man put Woody in the boot of his car.

Buzz couldn't let Woody be taken away, so he jumped out of the window and slid down the drainpipe, racing to rescue his friend. But he was too late.

All Buzz saw was a number plate, LZTYBRN, and a few feathers floating in the air as the car sped away.

The strange man took Woody to a high-rise apartment and put him inside a glass case. Then, to Woody's surprise, the toy-napper put on a chicken suit! He spoke to someone on the phone, then glanced at Woody and chuckled. "You, my little cowboy friend, are gonna make me big buck-buck-bucks!" he laughed.

Once he was alone, Woody ran to the door, trying to escape. But it was no use. He was trapped!

POP! A box suddenly burst open and Woody was knocked off his feet by a galloping toy horse.

"Yee-haw! It's really you!" shouted a cowgirl as she gave Woody a big hug.

The cowgirl said her name was Jessie and the horse was Bullseye. Then she introduced the Prospector, a mint-condition toy who had never been out of his box. All of them were thrilled to see Woody.

"We've waited countless years for this day," said the Prospector.

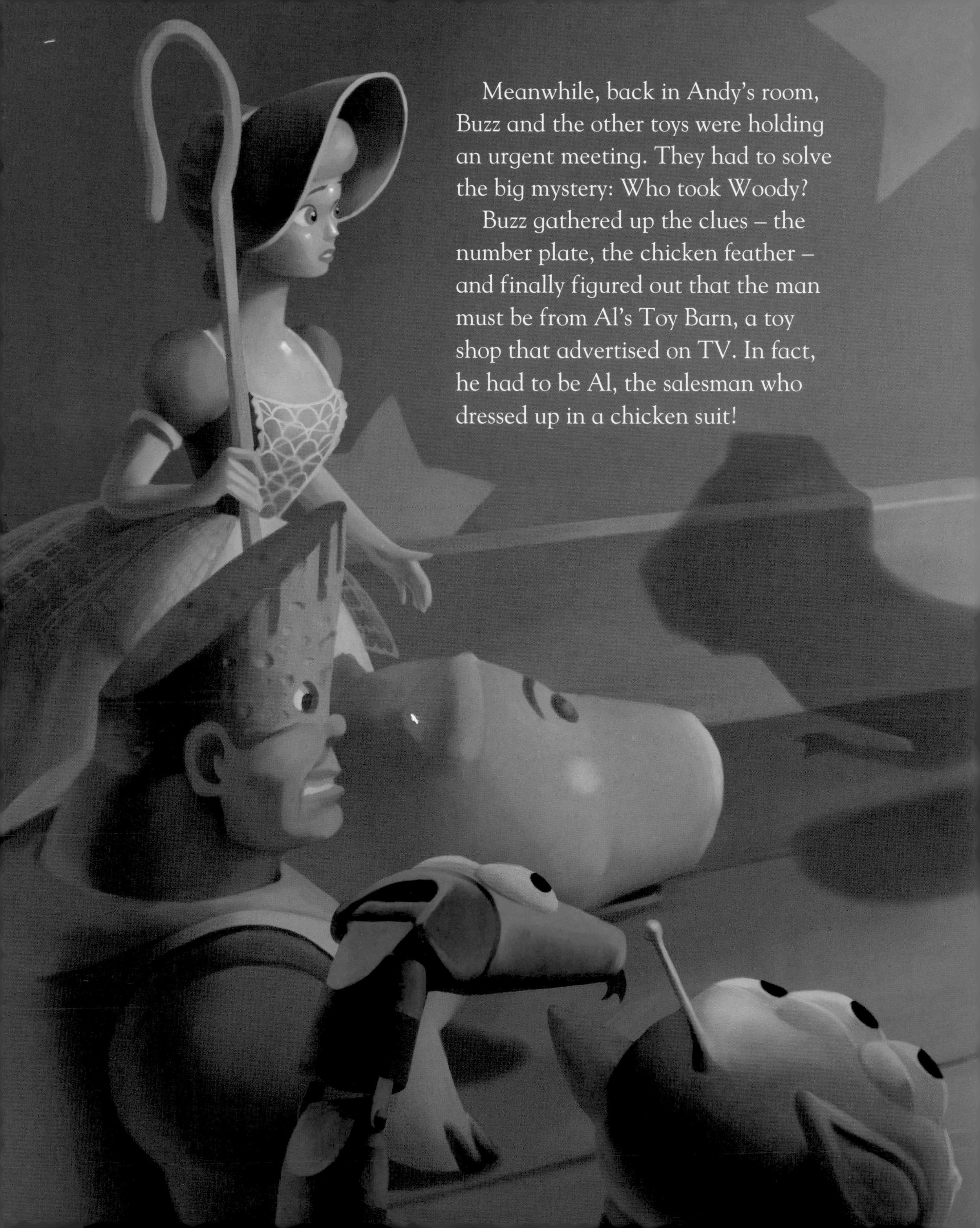

Meanwhile, back in Andy's room, Buzz and the other toys were holding an urgent meeting. They had to solve the big mystery: Who took Woody?

Buzz gathered up the clues – the number plate, the chicken feather – and finally figured out that the man must be from Al's Toy Barn, a toy shop that advertised on TV. In fact, he had to be Al, the salesman who dressed up in a chicken suit!

MAGIC Etch A

But now that they knew who the culprit was, what could the toys do?

"Woody once risked his life to save me," Buzz told the others. "I couldn't call myself his friend if I weren't willing to do the same."

Buzz decided to lead a rescue party to the toy shop to see if they could find Woody. Together, with a little help from Slinky, they jumped off the roof. "To Al's Toy Barn and beyond!" Buzz cried.

At Al's apartment, Woody couldn't understand how the other toys recognized him. "How do you know my name?" he asked.

"Why, you don't know who you are, do you?" the Prospector said.

Bullseye turned up the lights to reveal that the room was filled with items carrying Woody's picture: posters, magazines, lunchboxes, plates and toys. Woody couldn't believe his eyes!

Then Jessie showed Woody an old television show, *Woody's Roundup.* Woody was the star!

Woody laughed as he, Jessie and Bullseye explored all the memorabilia from *Woody's Roundup*.

"Now it's on to the museum!" the Prospector exclaimed.

"What museum?" Woody stopped in confusion.

The Prospector explained that the *Roundup* toys had become valuable collectibles. Al planned to sell the Prospector, Jessie, Bullseye and Woody, as a set, to a Japanese museum for a lot of money.

By early morning, Buzz and his rescue team had almost reached Al's Toy Barn. They just needed to cross one last, very busy, road.

Luckily, Buzz noticed a pile of orange traffic cones. He told everyone to grab one and then, slowly, they walked out into the traffic, hiding under the cones.

Soon, the road was filled with skidding, honking, crashing cars, all trying to avoid the strange, moving traffic cones! But the toys barely noticed. They had arrived at Al's Toy Barn.

Inside Al's Toy Barn, aisles of shiny new toys stretched into the distance. Everyone looked up in awe – how would they ever find Woody here?

The only one who didn't seem worried was Rex, who had picked up a book on how to defeat the evil Emperor Zurg from the Buzz Lightyear video game. Rex loved playing the game and desperately wanted to beat Buzz's arch-enemy. Rex couldn't stop reading, even as the toys spread out to search for Woody.

At the same time, up in Al's apartment, an old man had arrived to work on Woody.

The man opened a wooden case with special trays and drawers that were full of toy parts and doll paint. Then he started Woody's makeover.

He cleaned Woody's eyes and ears and repainted the top of the cowboy's head, where the paint had worn away. He even polished Woody's boots. Best of all, he sewed the rip in Woody's arm.

Al was thrilled. "He's just like new!"

BUZZ
SPACE

Meanwhile, Buzz was wandering the aisles of Al's Toy Barn. He turned a corner and discovered an aisle full of brand-new, updated Buzz Lightyear toys. He gasped in admiration at their fancy new utility belts.

As Buzz reached out to touch one of the belts, a hand suddenly clamped onto his wrist. It was a new Buzz Lightyear, who thought he'd caught a rogue space ranger! Quickly, New Buzz tied Andy's Buzz into a box and set it on the shelf. Then New Buzz ran to join Andy's toys – and not one of them realized they'd left the real Buzz behind!

The real Buzz struggled free from the box just in time to see Al carrying his friends out the front door – they had sneaked inside Al's bag! Racing to catch up, Buzz crashed into the automatic doors. To make the doors reopen, Buzz knocked a nearby pile of toy boxes onto the sensor mat. One box got stuck between the doors as Buzz ran off. Opening and closing, the doors hit the box over and over. At last, it popped open, and a dark figure rose up. It was the evil Emperor Zurg! He took one look at Buzz and growled, "Destroy Buzz Lightyear!"

EVIL EMPEROR
ZURG
ARCH ENEMY OF

Back at Al's apartment, Woody told Jessie that he couldn't go to the toy museum because he had to get back to Andy. He knew the best thing about being a toy was being loved by your owner.

Jessie sadly explained that she had once had an owner, too – a wonderful little girl named Emily, who used to play with her all the time. Jessie smiled as she remembered the wonderful times they had spent together....

But as Emily grew up, she played with Jessie less and less. Finally, she abandoned Jessie.

"You never forget kids like Emily or Andy," said Jessie. "But they forget you."

Woody began to worry that Andy would forget about him one day, too.

Outside, the toys had hoped to hitch a ride, hidden in Al's bag, to wherever Woody was being kept. But at his apartment building, Al jumped out of the car, leaving his bag behind – and the toys, too.

"No time to lose!" New Buzz shouted. Quickly, he led everyone into the building through an air vent. Then, because he thought he was a real space ranger, he tried to fly up to the top floor! Luckily, the lift came by just in time and carried everyone up instead.

Sneaking through the vents, the toys finally reached Al's apartment.

They charged into the room, knocking down Jessie and Bullseye, then grabbed Woody and ran. Everything was very chaotic and confusing – especially when the real Buzz showed up, too!

Finally, things got sorted out and everyone figured out who was who. But that still left one big problem....

"Woody, you're in danger here," said Buzz. He knew that Al wanted to send Woody to Japan. "We need to leave now."

ANDY

But Woody didn't want to leave. The *Roundup* gang needed him to make a complete set for the museum. Besides, what if Andy didn't want Woody any more? Al had fixed Woody's ripped shoulder, but what if he broke again?

"You're a toy!" Buzz said. "Life's only worth living if you're being loved by a kid."

"This is my only chance," Woody protested.

"To do what?" Buzz replied. "To watch kids from behind glass and never be loved again? Some life."

Sadly, Buzz left Woody behind, leading Andy's toys towards home.

Soon, though, Woody realized Buzz was right – he belonged with Andy. He ran to the vent and called for his friends to return. Then he turned to the *Roundup* gang. "Come with me," he said. "Andy will play with all of us, I know it!"

Jessie and Bullseye were excited ... but the Prospector blocked their path! After a lifetime in his box, he was determined to go to the museum. "And no hand-me-down cowboy doll is gonna mess it up for me now!" he shouted.

Suddenly, they heard footsteps – Al was coming!

Al packed Woody and the *Roundup* gang into a case and dashed out of the door and into a lift. He was late for his flight to Japan.

"Quick!" Buzz shouted, leading Andy's toys to the roof of the lift. But Emperor Zurg blocked their path!

As Zurg attacked the group with his blaster, Rex turned away, terrified – and accidentally knocked Zurg off the lift with his tail!

"I did it! I finally defeated Zurg!" Rex cried happily.

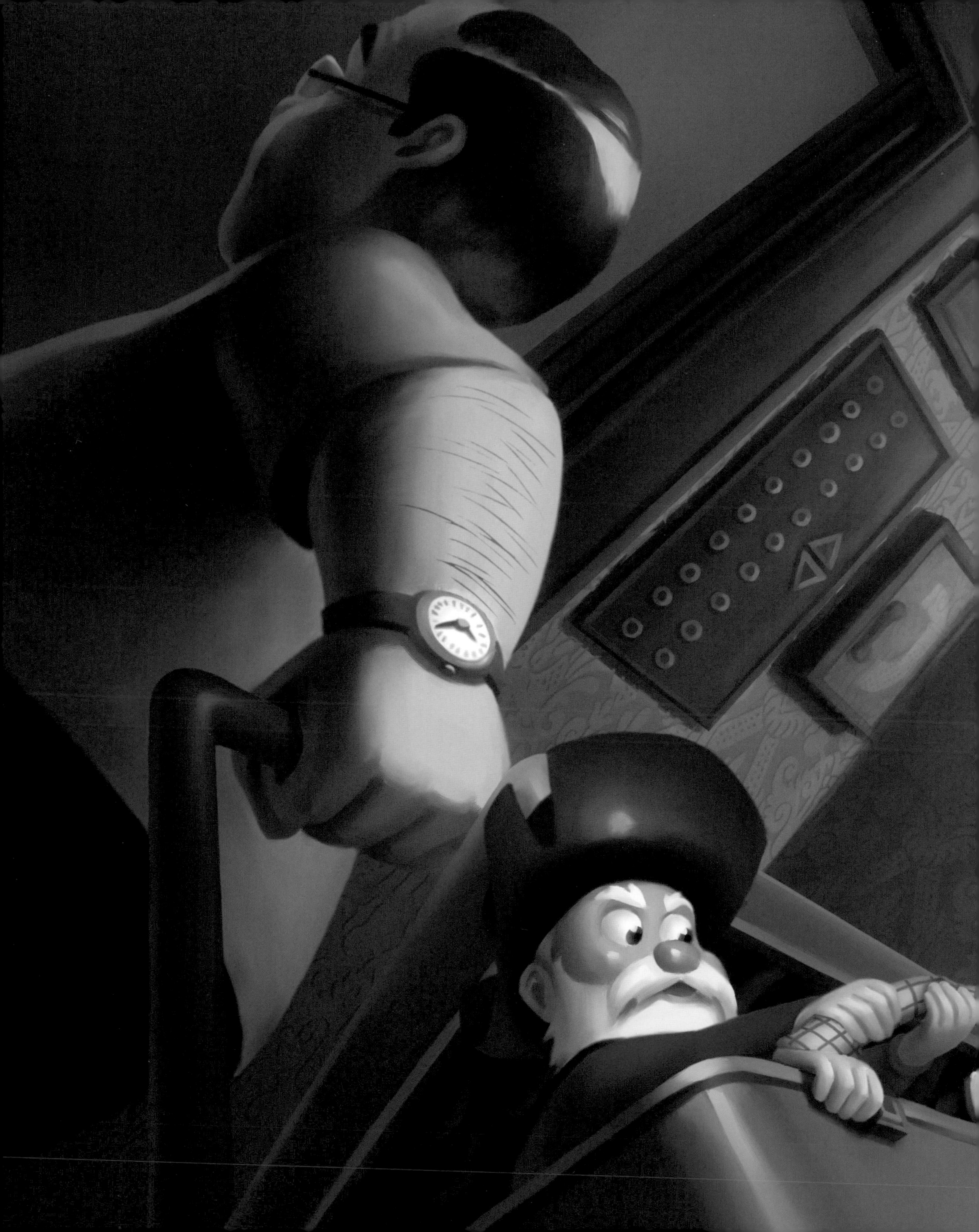

The moment Zurg was gone, the toys rushed to the lift's emergency hatch. Looking down, they saw Al, still inside.

Buzz held on to Slinky's back legs and the dog toy stretched down to Al's case. Swinging closer, he undid the latches and grabbed hold of Woody's arms.

But then, the Prospector popped up – and pulled Woody back down! A moment later, the lift doors opened on the ground floor. Al hurried outside, with the *Roundup* gang still inside his case.

Andy's toys sprinted into the car park, but Al had already jumped into his car and driven off. How would they rescue Woody now?

Luckily, the toys spotted an empty Pizza Planet truck nearby. Maybe they could use the truck to follow Al and Woody.

The real Buzz Lightyear asked New Buzz if he wanted to come.

"No," replied the deluded space toy. "I have a lot of catching up to do with my dad." Now he thought that Zurg was his father!

Zurg had escaped the fall from the lift unharmed. He shot a ball at New Buzz, who caught it and threw it back. "Good throw, son," Zurg cried.

The real Buzz smiled and ran towards his friends.

"Does anyone know how to drive?" Rex asked as the toys hopped into the Pizza Planet truck.

Buzz gave everyone a job to do. He would steer, while Slinky Dog pushed the pedals. Rex kept his eye on Al's car and yelled out directions.

"He's at the red light!" Rex shouted. "We can catch him!"

Soon they were swerving through traffic, hot on the trail of Al's car.

Driving wildly, Buzz and the gang followed Al right to the airport entrance. But the toys couldn't walk openly through the crowd. Luckily, Buzz spotted a pet carrier. The toys piled inside, sticking their legs through the bottom so they could walk. Moving as quickly as they dared, the group moved through the airport, following Al and his green case.

Still in the pet carrier, Andy's toys climbed onto the luggage conveyor belt, following Al's green suitcase.

"Once we go through, we just need to find that case," Buzz explained, nodding at the door to the baggage area.

The toys gasped as they entered a room. Bags and suitcases and boxes headed off in all different directions.

Buzz finally found Al's case, but when he opened it – POW! – the Prospector jumped out and punched Buzz.

"Hey! No one does that to my friend," Woody yelled, tackling the Prospector.

With his pickaxe, the Prospector ripped Woody's shoulder open again and was about to drag Woody back into the case when Andy's toys arrived, just in time.

Jessie and Bullseye were still trapped inside Al's case. The little horse kicked free as the conveyor belt carried them outside, but Jessie was stuck!

"Ride like the wind, Bullseye!" Woody yelled as he and Buzz jumped on Bullseye's back. They raced over the tarmac, chasing the luggage truck.

Woody finally scrambled onto the truck, but by then the green case was already being loaded into a plane. Woody hid inside another suitcase and was tossed onto the plane, too.

Searching through the cargo hold, Woody found the scared cowgirl. "C'mon, Jess," he said. "It's time to take you home."

Just then, the plane's doors closed. They were stuck inside!

Desperate, they crawled through a hatch, down to the plane's wheels. The plane was already speeding down the runway – Woody and Jessie could barely hold on! Then Woody slipped! Jessie caught him just in time, but his shoulder was starting to rip even more.

Twirling his pull-string, Woody tried a daring trick. First he lassoed a bolt on the wheels. Then he grabbed Jessie's hand and ...

... together, they swung towards the ground!

As the two hurtled down and under the plane, Woody's pull-string unhooked from the aeroplane bolt – throwing them right to Buzz, who was galloping along on Bullseye! Everyone was safe.

Watching the plane take off into the sky, Woody, Jessie, Buzz and Bullseye danced and cheered.

"That was definitely Woody's finest hour!" cried Jessie.

And what happened to the Prospector? In the airport, Woody and Buzz had strapped the Prospector to a pink backpack – which belonged to an excited little girl who couldn't wait to play with a new doll. The Prospector wouldn't be in perfect condition much longer!

When Andy arrived home from Cowboy Camp, he was surprised by what he found.

"New toys!" he cried. "Thanks, Mum!"

Jessie and Bullseye had joined all his favourites, welcoming him home. Andy couldn't wait to play with everyone ... just as soon as he had sewn up Woody's shoulder.

Someday Andy would grow up – and maybe he wouldn't always play with toys – but Woody and Buzz knew there was no place they would rather be.

Besides, they would always have each other ... for infinity and beyond!